For Jessica.

Pioneer. Feminist. Sister.

www.mascotbooks.com

The Boy with the Rainbow Heart

Text & Illustrations copyright © 2017 by William Mason

Mason, William S.
The Boy with the Rainbow Heart / by William Mason; illustrated by William Mason & Coraline Tran

p. cm.

Summary: A boy with a rainbow heart turns the town of Gray into the town of Shine by being himself.
[1. Children's picture book—Fiction. 2. Children's Diversity—Fiction. 3. Diversity—Fiction.]
Cataloging-in-Publication details are available from the Library Congress.
The text type is Hank BT. The illustrations are mixed media, including acrylic, pen and ink, and 2-D art.
Designer: Cody Weiler | Editor: Kate Quinlivan Mason

Printed in the U.S.A.
Published by Mascot Books
CPSIA Code: PRT1017A
First Edition 10 9 8 7 6 5 4 3 2 1
ISBN: 978-0-692-93553-8
WPC0310

SPONSORED IN PART BY

The Boy
WITH THE
Rainbow Heart

WRITTEN BY

William S. Mason III

ILLUSTRATED BY

Coraline Tran

There once was a boy with a rainbow heart.

He lived in the town of Gray.

And as he grew up,
everything the boy touched
filled with colorful rays!

But the gray town was sad,
and so shined through
the colors of black and blue.

The town lived in fear, and the people were scared of any heart colored different than theirs.

But the boy remained happy
and merry and light.
And his heart was full,
and always shined bright.

There once was a boy with a rainbow heart.

He wore his colors on his sleeves.

For each day that passed,
the boy's rays were cast,
and the town's gray began to leave.

It started with yellow,
then blue, red, and green,
and soon the town shined like a beam!

The boy's heart took over,
and made the town glow,
and only bright colors
were left to flow.

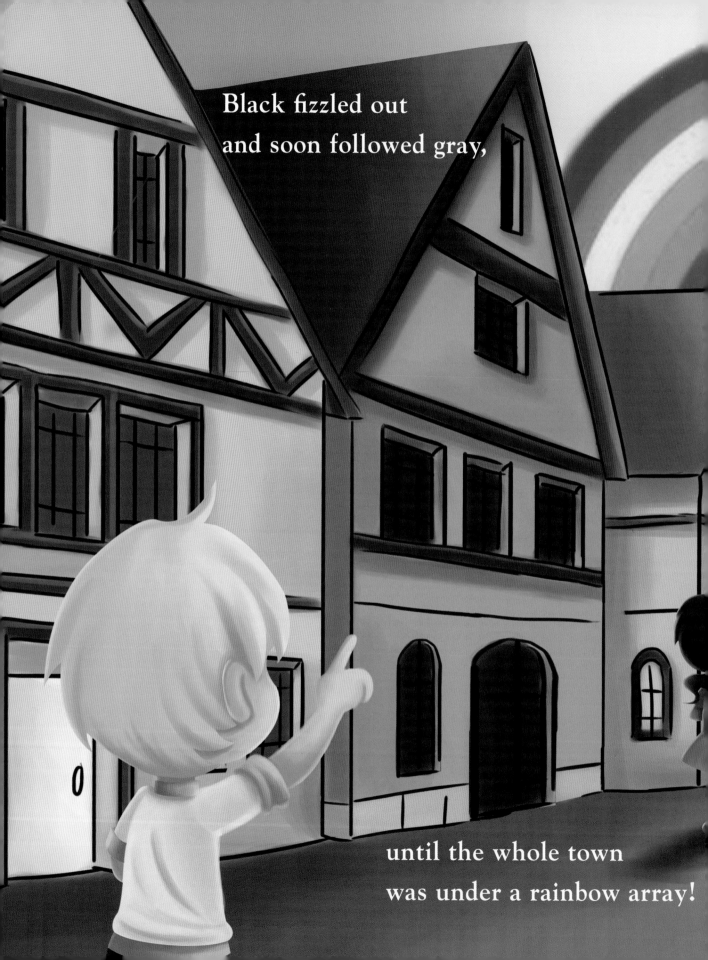

Black fizzled out
and soon followed gray,

until the whole town
was under a rainbow array!

The townspeople changed too,
and so did their hearts.
With each new color,
their fears fell apart.

The boy's love for all people
changed their hearts for good.
And the town of Gray's
people soon understood.

Once a heart has true love,
it doesn't matter its shine,
a heart is always perfect,
as long as it's kind.

There once was a boy with a rainbow heart.

Through the power of love,
his heart changed the town's sign.

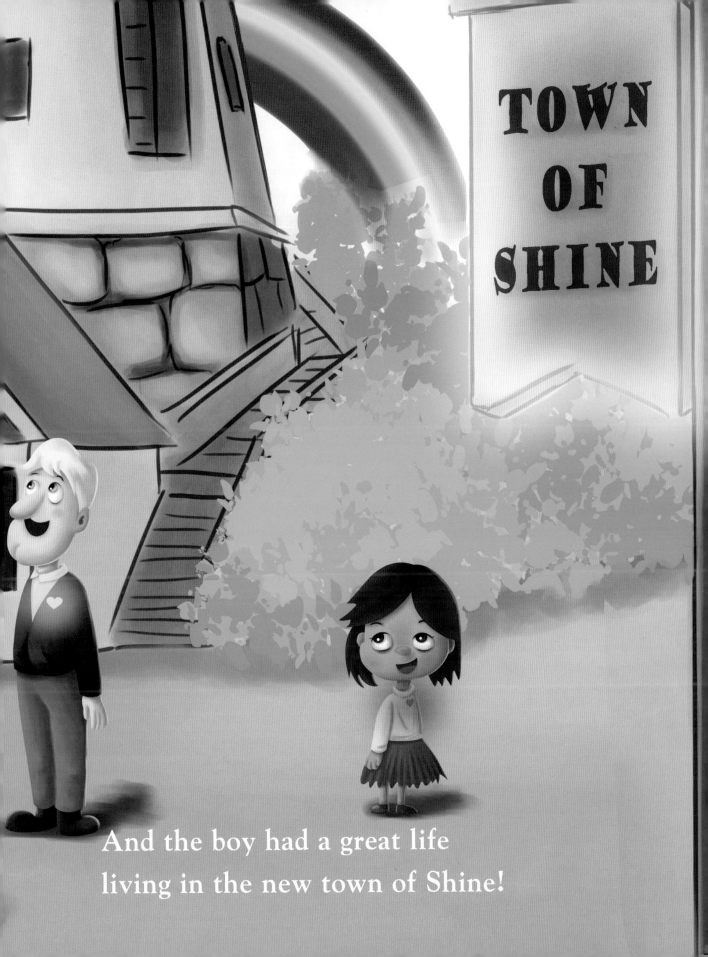

And the boy had a great life
living in the new town of Shine!